SONNY'S BIRTHDAY PRIZE

Lisa Stubbs

Piccadilly Press • London

When Sonny was leaving playgroup his friend Katie gave him an invitation to her birthday party on Saturday.
"Thank you," said Sonny.

As soon as he got home, Sonny made Katie a card. Gran had already knitted a scarf, which she wrapped up for Katie's present.

When Saturday came, Sonny was very excited. He eagerly washed his face and brushed his beak ready for Katie's party.

At the party, Sonny gave Katie her
card and present. "They're brilliant,"
said Katie.
Sonny saw all her wonderful presents and
wished that just one was for him.

They all sat down to a birthday tea. They ate banana sandwiches, jelly and ice cream. When Katie blew out the candles on the birthday cake, everyone sang "Happy Birthday".

After tea, Katie's dad
organised the party games.
They played Musical Statues . . .

Pin the Tail on the Donkey . . .

and Pass the Parcel.

Sonny was sad when he didn't
win any of the games.

Then they played Hide and Seek. Katie started counting, "1 . . . 2 . . . 3 . . . Coming, ready or not."

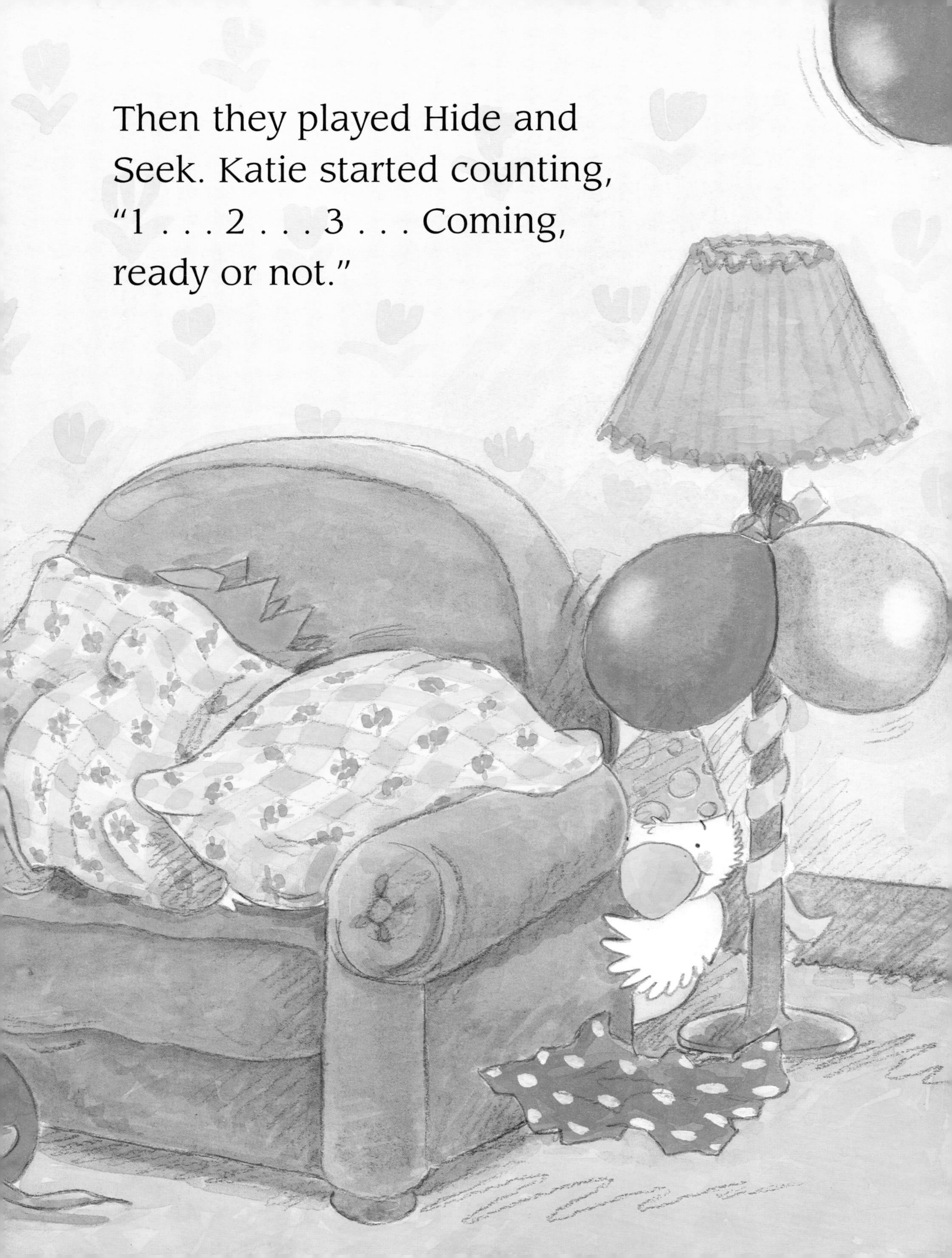

"Found you!"

"I can
see
you!"

It was soon time for the
children to go home. Katie had
found all of them – except Sonny.
"Where *is* Sonny?"
asked Grandma.

Everyone looked for Sonny while Katie's dad tidied up in the kitchen.

"He's here!" shouted Katie's dad, pointing at the wash basket.

Sonny won first prize for
finding the best ever hiding place!